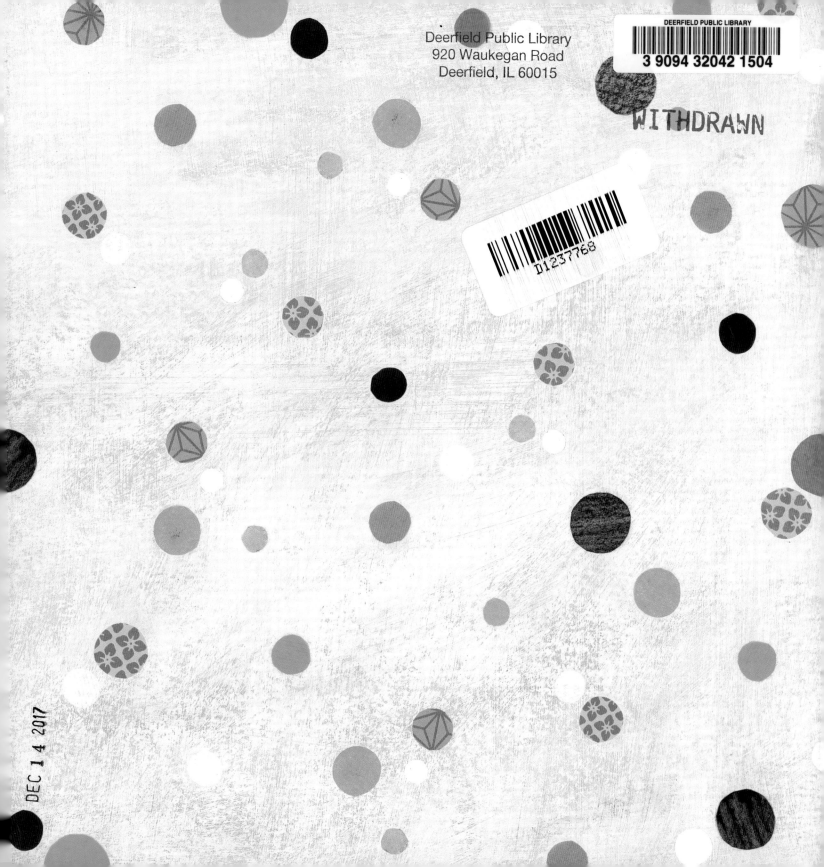

Bear Hug
Somos8 Series

© Text: Susanna Isern, 2016
© Illustration: Betania Zacarias, 2016
© Edition: NubeOcho, 2017
www.nubeocho.com – info@nubeocho.com

Original title: *Abrazo de Oso*
English translation: Ben Dawlatly
Text editing: Rebecca Packard

Distributed in the United States by
Consortium Book Sales & Distribution

First edition: 2017
ISBN: 978-84-946333-3-1

Printed in China by Asia Pacific Offset,
respecting international labor standards.

BEAR HUG

Susanna Isern
Betania Zacarias

Natuk lived far north, where visits from the sun
were fleeting, and the starry, moonlit nights
seemed to go on forever.

One afternoon, while she was strolling across
the frozen sea ice, she found a tiny white bear
curled up in a little ball.

The little bear was alone; there was nobody around for miles. He was so small that he could hardly open his eyes. Without giving it a second thought, Natuk cradled him in her arms. "I'll help you find your mommy," she whispered to him.

But despite searching high and low, she couldn't find the little bear's mother anywhere.
"Let's go home. It's warm there," said Natuk when she saw that he was trembling. She snuggled him close to her body.

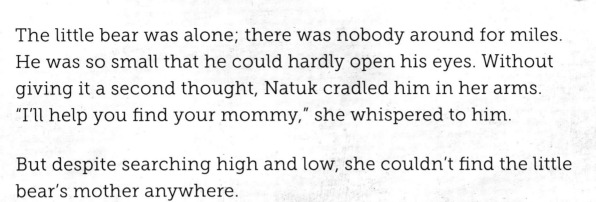

That night, the little bear couldn't stop shivering, so Natuk slept next to him.

By the next morning he was less scared, but he was very hungry. The little girl gave him some tuna flakes and fresh water. He showed his gratitude by licking her on the cheek and giving her a mini bear hug.

That night, and every night from then on, Natuk and the bear slept in the same bed.

As time passed, White Bear grew and turned into a huge, strong animal. He and Natuk were inseparable.

Together they would wander across the icy plains and glide down glaciers as if they were giant slides. They would never get bored of teasing the penguins and seals peacefully napping in the rays of the distant sun.

One night while the Eskimos were sleeping, their stockpile of fish was raided. It had taken them a lot of effort to catch all that fish, and they were storing it for hard times.

When they woke up and saw what had happened, they were all very worried. The village elder let his suspicions be known right away.

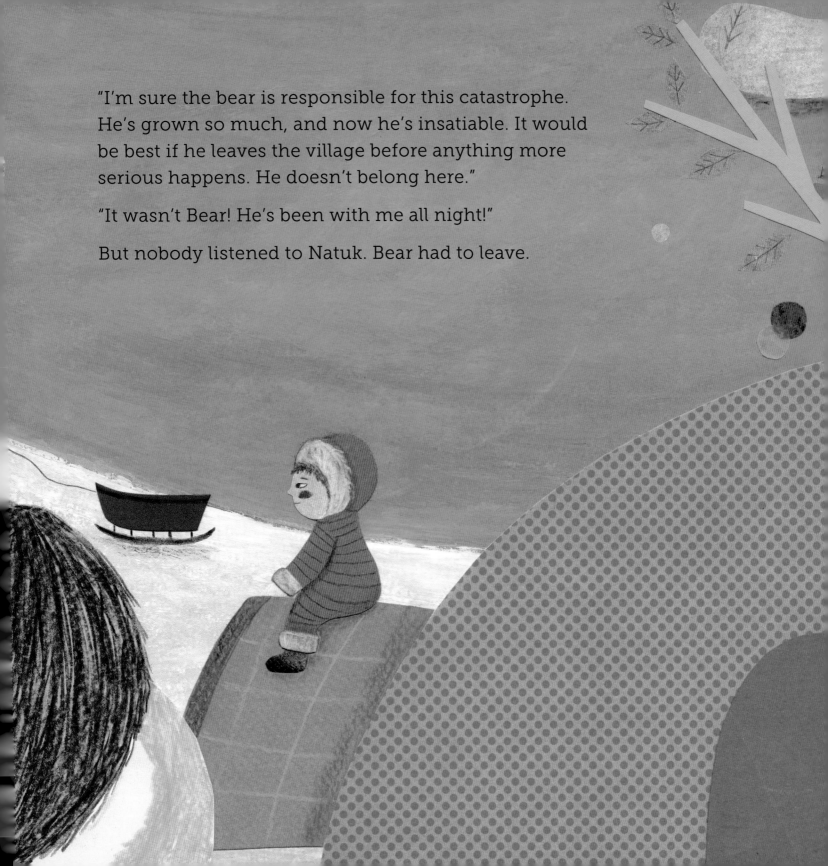

"I'm sure the bear is responsible for this catastrophe. He's grown so much, and now he's insatiable. It would be best if he leaves the village before anything more serious happens. He doesn't belong here."

"It wasn't Bear! He's been with me all night!"

But nobody listened to Natuk. Bear had to leave.

That same morning, Natuk and White Bear left the village. They walked for hours and hours. When they were far enough away, they stopped.

The little girl looked into her best friend's eyes. They were deep and black, and they seemed to be shining more than usual. Then she hugged him around the neck to say goodbye while she cried frozen tears.
"Take care of yourself, buddy. I'll never forget you."

And, for the first time in what seemed like forever, their paths went in different directions.

Once White Bear had gone, Natuk's days were very sad. She couldn't stop thinking about her friend. She wondered where he was and if he was okay. She missed him so much.

So one morning, before dawn, she snuck out to find him.

When Natuk got to the place she'd last seen Bear, the sun had already come out. She had a look around to see if she could see any trace of him. She shouted as loud as she could:

"BEAR!"

But it was as if the earth had swallowed Bear up. The little girl decided to take her search into desolate, unknown lands.

At that time of year, the days were very short, and Natuk was surprised when night suddenly arrived along with a powerful storm.

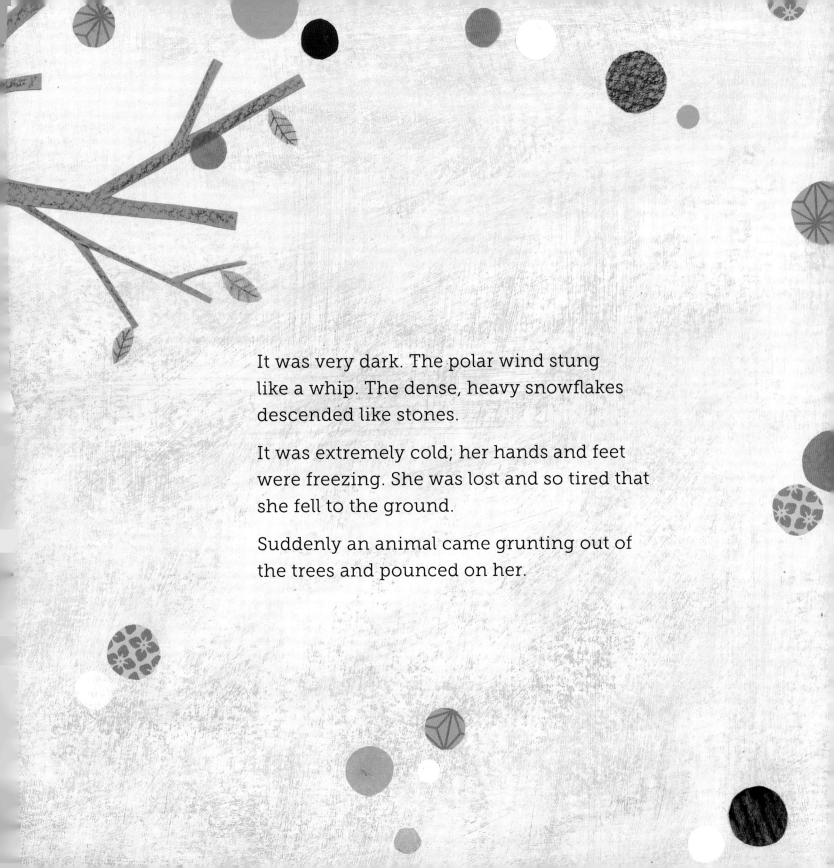

It was very dark. The polar wind stung
like a whip. The dense, heavy snowflakes
descended like stones.

It was extremely cold; her hands and feet
were freezing. She was lost and so tired that
she fell to the ground.

Suddenly an animal came grunting out of
the trees and pounced on her.

It was White Bear! He'd found her!
Bear wrapped his giant body around
Natuk and hugged her tightly to
protect her all night.

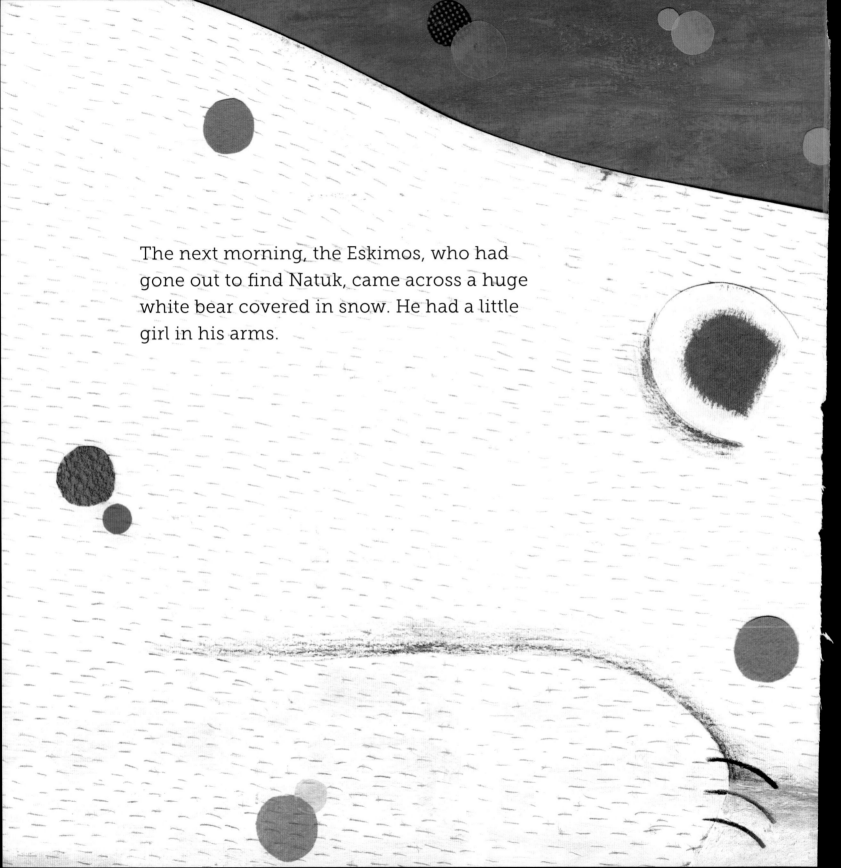

The next morning, the Eskimos, who had gone out to find Natuk, came across a huge white bear covered in snow. He had a little girl in his arms.

Natuk woke up at that very moment. When she saw them, she clung to Bear with all her might.

"Bear saved my life! Bear saved my life!" she shouted.

"We know. You don't need to worry. We know it was the wolves that stole the fish. And since Bear hasn't been around, they get into the village much more easily. We would like him to come back to protect us."

Natuk and White Bear were together again.
They loved racing with the Arctic hares,
fishing for dreams in the sea and counting
the shooting stars on moonless nights.

And when Natuk was sad, cold or scared, or when it was stormy, she could always count on one of his hugs... a Bear hug.